Elizabeth Akers

Rock me to Sleep, Mother

Elizabeth Akers

Rock me to Sleep, Mother

ISBN/EAN: 9783743480889

Manufactured in Europe, USA, Canada, Australia, Japa

Cover: Foto ©Andreas Hilbeck / pixelio.de

Manufactured and distributed by brebook publishing software
(www.brebook.com)

Elizabeth Akers

Rock me to Sleep, Mother

Rock Me to Sleep, Mother.

BY

ELIZABETH AKERS ALLEN.

ILLUSTRATED.

BOSTON:

PUBLISHED BY ESTES AND LAURIAT.

1883.

UNIVERSITY PRESS:
JOHN WILSON & SON, CAMBRIDGE.

LIST OF ILLUSTRATIONS

Drawn and Engraved under the supervision of

GEORGE T. ANDREW.

———◆———

ARTISTS:

S. G. McCUTCHEON.   JESSIE CURTIS SHEPHERD.

F. S. CHURCH.   W. L. TAYLOR.

E. H. GARRETT.   FRANCIS MILLER.

———◆———

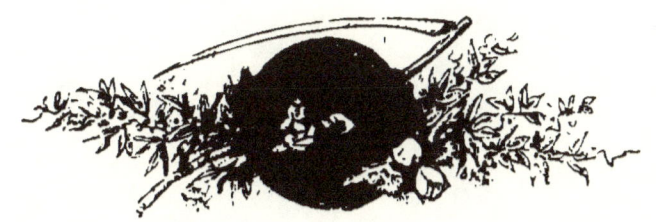

ROCK ME TO SLEEP, MOTHER

BACKWARD, turn backward, O Time, in your
    flight,
Make me a child again, just for to-night !
Mother, come back from the echoless shore,
Take me again to your heart, as of yore ;
Kiss from my forehead the furrows of care,
Smooth the few silver threads out of my hair,
Over my slumbers your loving watch keep, —
Rock me to sleep, mother, rock me to sleep.

Backward, flow backward, O tide of the years !
I am so weary of toil and of tears, —
Toil without recompense, tears all in vain,
Take them and give me my childhood again ;
I have grown weary of dust and decay,
Weary of flinging my soul-wealth away,
Weary of sowing for others to reap, —
Rock me to sleep, mother, rock me to sleep.

Tired of the hollow, the base, the untrue,
Mother, O mother, my heart calls for you ;
Many a summer the grass has grown green,
Blossomed and faded, our faces between,
Yet, with strong yearning and passionate pain,
Long I to-night for your presence again.
Come from the silence so long and so deep, —
Rock me to sleep, mother, rock me to sleep.

Over my heart, in the days that are flown,
No love like mother-love ever has shone ;
No other worship abides and endures
Faithful, unselfish, and patient, like yours ;
None like a mother can charm away pain
From the sick soul and the world-weary brain.
Slumber's soft calms o'er my heavy lids creep, —
Rock me to sleep, mother, rock me to sleep.

Come, let your brown hair, just lighted with
    gold,
Fall on your shoulders again, as of old ;
Let it drop over my forehead to-night,
Shading my faint eyes away from the light,
For with its sunny-edged shadows once more,
Haply will throng the sweet visions of yore ;
Lovingly, softly, its bright billows sweep, —
Rock me to sleep, mother, rock me to sleep.

Mother, dear mother, the years have been long,
Since I last listened your lullaby song ;
Sing, then, and unto my soul it shall seem
Womanhood's years have been only a dream.
Clasped to your heart in a loving embrace,
With your light lashes just sweeping my face,
Never hereafter to wake or to weep, —
Rock me to sleep, mother, rock me to sleep.

ROCK ME TO SLEEP, MOTHER.

BACKWARD, turn backward, O Time, in your flight,
Make me a child again, just for to-night!
Mother, come back from the echoless shore,
Take me again to your heart, as of yore;
Kiss from my forehead the furrows of care,
Smooth the few silver threads out of my hair,

" Mother, come back from the echoless shore."

Over my slumbers your loving watch keep, —
Rock me to sleep, mother, rock me to sleep.

"*I am so weary of toil and of tears.*"

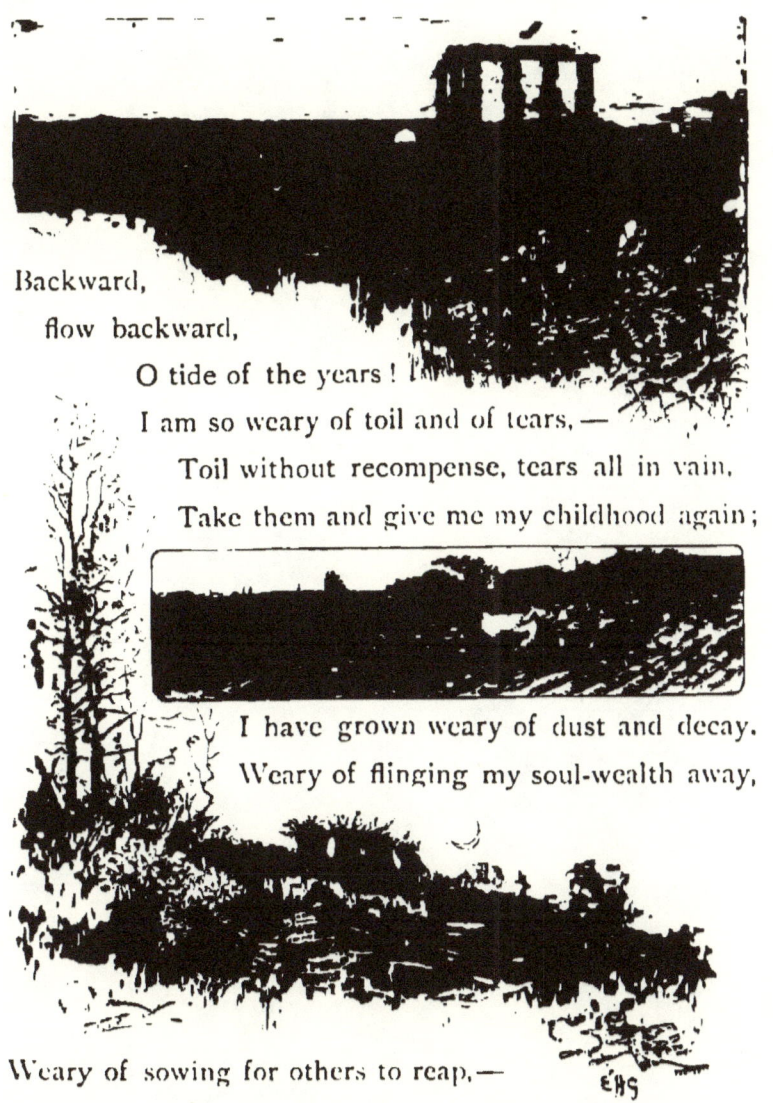

Backward,

  flow backward,

    O tide of the years!

    I am so weary of toil and of tears, —

      Toil without recompense, tears all in vain,

      Take them and give me my childhood again;

      I have grown weary of dust and decay.

      Weary of flinging my soul-wealth away,

Weary of sowing for others to reap, —

Rock me to sleep, mother, rock me to sleep.

"Many a summer the grass has grown green."

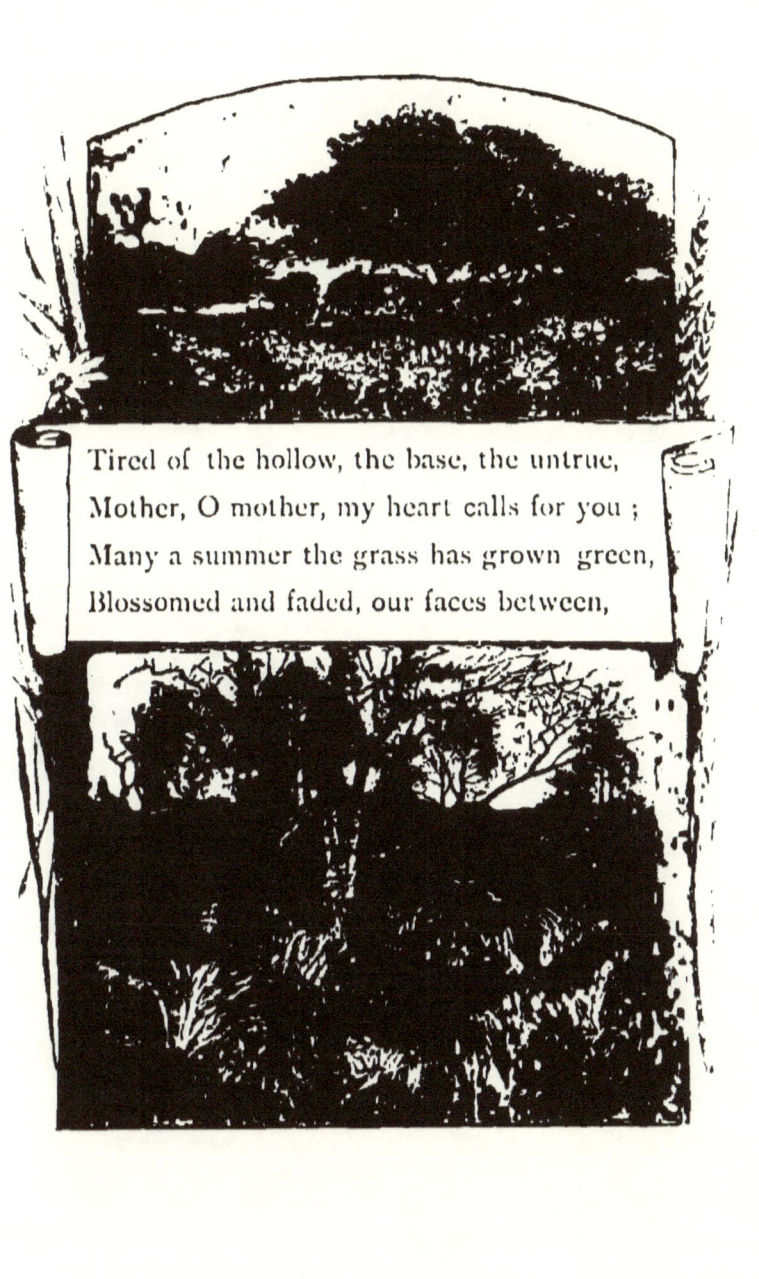

Tired of the hollow, the base, the untrue,
Mother, O mother, my heart calls for you ;
Many a summer the grass has grown green,
Blossomed and faded, our faces between,

Yet, with strong yearning and passionate pain,
Long I to-night for your presence again.

Come from the silence so long and so deep,-
Rock me to sleep mother, rock me to sleep.

"No love like mother-love ever has shone."

Over my heart, in the days that are flown,
No love like mother-love ever has shone;

No other worship abides and endures
Faithful, unselfish, and patient, like yours;
None like a mother can charm away pain
From the sick soul and the world-weary brain.
Slumber's soft calms o'er my heavy lids creep, —
Rock me to sleep, mother, rock me to sleep.

"Haply will throng the sweet visions of yore."

Come, let your brown hair, just lighted with gold,
Fall on your shoulders again, as of old;

Let it drop over my forehead to-night,
Shading my faint eyes away from the light,

or with its sunny-edged shadows once more,
Haply will throng the sweet visions of yore;
Lovingly, softly, its bright
billows sweep, —
Rock me to sleep, mother,
rock me to sleep.

"Since I last listen'd your lullaby song."

Mother, dear mother, the years have been long,
Since I last listened your lullaby song;
Sing, then, and unto my soul it shall seem
Womanhood's years have been only a dream.
Clasped to your heart in a loving embrace,
With your light lashes just sweeping my face,
Never hereafter to wake or to weep, —
Rock me to sleep, mother, rock me to sleep.